My Left Hand

By Alan Trussell-Cullen
Illustrated by Lisa Coutts

Chapter 1

Everything Was Going So Well – and Then . . .

Donna's two brothers hold their spoon in their right hand when they eat – but not Donna. When the children in Donna's class play ball games, everyone throws the ball with their right hand – but not Donna. When the children in Donna's class are writing stories, they all hold their pencils in their right hand – but not Donna.

That's because Donna is left-handed.

Donna eats with her left hand, throws a ball with her left hand and writes with her left hand. In fact, Donna does everything with her left hand – except shake hands. That's because everyone else uses their right hand, and if she used her left, all the right-handers would get very muddled!

When Donna was a baby, her parents hadn't noticed she was left-handed until one day her aunty came to visit.

"You know young Donna is left-handed?" she said to Donna's mum.

"Is she?" Mum said. "I guess she's just like me."

Donna's mum was left-handed too. Her dad was right-handed. Donna's two brothers took after their father, but Donna took after her mother.

"I guess that makes Donna a little bit special," Mum said to Donna's aunty.

Donna liked being a little bit special. And she liked eating with her left hand because it felt right. She liked throwing a ball with her left hand because the ball always went where she wanted it to go. And as for writing, she was one of the best story-writers in the class. So Donna felt really good about her left hand.

Well, she felt really good about it until a month ago. That was when she fell out of a tree and broke her arm – her left arm!

Chapter 2

The Bad News
Just Gets Worse . . .

Dad had to take Donna to the doctor. She had to have her arm x-rayed and put in plaster. The doctor showed Donna the x-ray. Donna asked if she could take the x-ray home so she could take it to school and show it to all the kids in her class. She wanted to see if anyone fainted! But the doctor said they had to keep it there so they could compare it with her arm when the break had healed.

That night, Donna had to eat her dinner with her right hand. Everything kept sliding off her fork, and when she did get something to stay on her fork, she kept missing her mouth and jabbing her cheek.

The next day at school, Donna made a big impression with her arm in plaster. Everyone wanted to know how she did it and whether it had hurt. Of course it had hurt terribly, but Donna said: "It didn't hurt a bit! I didn't even cry!" (That wasn't true!)

Everyone said "Wow!" and wanted to sign their name on her plaster.

But when the teacher took the class outside for a game, Donna had to throw the ball with her right hand. Her first throw went over the fence and everyone laughed. Her next throw nearly hit the teacher, and everyone laughed even more! Donna was now the worst thrower in the whole class!

Then it came time to write stories. Donna liked writing stories. She always had good ideas and wrote quickly as the ideas kept bobbing into her head. But her right hand couldn't keep up with her ideas, and no matter how hard she tried to keep her letters on the line, they seemed to jump up and down all over the place.

The next day it was the same. And the next. And the next. In fact, for four long weeks Donna struggled to make her right hand do what she wanted it to do.

Chapter 3

And Then It All Changed . . .

All of that changed when Donna went back to the doctor and had the plaster taken off.

That night she had no problem finding her mouth with her fork.

"Good job!" she told her left hand.

The following day, Donna took her x-rays to school to show the class. The children crowded round to look at them.

"Wow!" they said.

(Donna was a little disappointed when no one fainted.)

Then the teacher took the class outside for a game. Donna picked up the ball with her left hand and threw it. It went just where she wanted it to go! The other children clapped.

Later that day, the class began to write their stories. Donna knew what she was going to write about. She was going to write a story about a girl who is left-handed and falls out of a tree. She breaks her arm and has to do everything with her right hand!

For the first time in weeks, Donna's pencil seemed to keep up with her ideas. She wrote and wrote and wrote. She was so glad to have her left hand working properly again. (She thought her right hand was very pleased too!) And she knew what the title of her story was going to be: *My Left Hand!*